Pinned & Possessed: Erotic KO Wrestling Fantasies Vol. 1

By: Phantom Rose

Published by Phantom Rose

ISBN: 979-8-218-74467-0

Any form of wrestling, including fetish wrestling, should emphasize and prioritize safety through clear and concise communication, establishing safe words, as well as understanding and respecting boundaries always. Remember, ***SAFETY IS PARAMOUNT***

PREFACE

Fetish is powerful.

For many of us, these fantasies don't live in darkness—they live in vivid color. They're playful, sensual, mysterious, and deeply personal. I've always been fascinated by the unique blend of dominance, vulnerability, and slow surrender that comes with **limp, KO, and pin wrestling fantasies.**

Watching a strong, confident woman slowly fall limp, spread open, tongue out, completely under the control of another—it's a form of erotic performance that combines physicality with intense sensual energy.

But let me be clear: **this book is pure fantasy.**

All the scenarios within these pages are consensual creations between willing participants (fictional characters). I firmly believe that the best kink play—whether fantasy or reality—**thrives on mutual trust, communication, and safety.**

I wrote this book not just to turn you on (though I hope it does that plenty), but also to show that erotica can be both deeply arousing **and** deeply respectful of its players.

If you're a reader, a model, or a fellow creator in this space—I hope these stories spark ideas, desires, and maybe even open doors to your own unique adventures.

PROLOGUE

<u>The Arena of Submission</u>

There's a secret world beneath the surface of the wrestling scene.

Beyond the public shows and staged promos lies a private circuit—a place where matches aren't about titles or fame, but **control**.

Women meet in hidden gyms, private studios, and softly lit rooms.

Here, the rules change.

A pin isn't just a pin. It's a possession.

A KO isn't just an act. It's an invitation to explore **deep surrender**.

Stripping isn't humiliation—it's sensual unveiling.

In this world, dominant women strip, tease, sniff, fondle, spank, and grind their partners into limp, twitching submission. And those who surrender?

They do so willingly, drunk on the pleasure of being pinned, used, and adored as objects of erotic art.

This is the world you're about to enter.

Welcome to **Pinned & Possessed**.

INTRODUCTION

Welcome to Pinned & Possessed Vol. 1

You hold in your hands the first volume of what I hope becomes an ongoing series celebrating the art of **erotic domination through limp wrestling fantasies.**

Inside, you'll find a collection of five progressively more intense short stories. Each one explores different dynamics:

- Playful sparring between roommates.
- Power-shifting scenes between models and photographers.
- Sensual "auditions" for new submissive talent.
- Full-on private ring matches of stripping, sniffing, and grinding submission.

The stories were written to blend **ultra-kinky eroticism** with a consistent focus on **safety, consent, and trust.**

At the end of each story, you'll also find a brief set of **"Notes & Lessons"** that highlight how to enjoy these types of activities safely, offer sensual tips, and explore some of the mental, emotional, and even physical health benefits that come from this type of trust-based erotic play.

Whether you're reading for personal pleasure, professional curiosity, or creative inspiration—I hope this collection leaves you both aroused and empowered.

And yes—models, performers, and producers: consider this book my love letter to your work, your talents, and your bodies.

STORY 1 – THE JOBBER'S DOWNFALL (INTRO PREVIEW)

The lights overhead flickered into a seductive red as the ropes around the ring shimmered like a cage of desire. The arena was private—just the cameras, the mats, and two women who'd agreed to settle a score the only way they knew how.

Jenny, the rising starlet, cocky and bronzed, licked her lips as she bounced on her heels. Tight shorts hugged her hips, and a matching sports bra clung to her toned chest.

Across from her, **Jessie**, the veteran—thick thighs, dark eyes, a grin like she already knew how this would end. Jessie wore only knee-high boots and a black thong-bodysuit that left little to the imagination.

"Ready to go down, little jobber?" Jessie purred.

Jenny smirked. "Let's see who's still conscious at the end."

What followed was a slow, sensual beatdown—Jessie didn't just want to win. She wanted to break her. Each DDT, each belly splash, each breathy KO whisper was layered with teasing. Jenny's resistance melted with every hold, every straddle, every sniff of her sweat-slicked skin.

By the end, Jenny lay **limp, spread-eagle**, tongue hanging out, her bra tossed aside, panties barely hanging on. Jessie sat on her belly, **dry humping her softly**, fingers sliding over her inner thighs, eyes half-lidded.

"Mmm... musty little thing," she whispered, sniffing Jenny's armpit and giggling.

Jenny twitched once. Then lay still.

Jessie grinned. **Pinned. Owned. Perfect.**

Story 1: The Jobber's Downfall

By Phantom Rose

POV: Omniscient voyeur – watching two women fall into a sensual, dominant rhythm.

The lights flickered crimson above the ring. No audience, no referees—just sweat, shadows, and two women with something to prove.

Jenny, golden-haired and smug, bounced in her corner. Her tight black sports bra hugged her chest, showing just a hint of sweat already forming. She was young. Cocky. Fast. But across the mat stood Jessie, seasoned and still as a predator. Her dark one-piece clung to her powerful curves like a second skin. Her thighs were thick with promise.

"Let's make this fun," Jessie purred, circling.

Jenny smirked. "Don't blink."

The bell never rang. They just lunged.

Within moments, Jenny's speed gave her the edge—ducking, diving, hitting a few quick holds. Jessie grinned through it, letting the jobber tire herself out. She was patient. She was planning.

Then came the shift.

A sudden belly splash drove the wind out of Jenny. She gasped. Her arms went slack. Jessie took her by the chin, smiling down into her wide eyes.

"Oh… you're soft now."

She hoisted her into a DDT—*bam.* Jenny hit the mat like a ragdoll, arms splayed, legs twitching.

"That's more like it."

Jessie straddled her waist and began the tease—fingers grazing the edge of Jenny's bra. She leaned in close… and *sniffed* her armpit.

"Mmm. Musty little jobber," she whispered. "You smell like fear and fun."

Jenny stirred faintly—too dazed to respond. Her tongue peeked out, eyes half-lidded.

Jessie unhooked the bra and tossed it aside. One hand cupped Jenny's breast; the other slowly slid between her legs.

"Let's get you pinned properly."

Another slam—a Pedigree—left Jenny limp. Jessie peeled her shorts down to reveal a soaked thong. Then she flipped her onto her back, *spread-eagle*, arms limp and twitching.

She licked her lips, lowered herself onto Jenny's hips, grinding gently. Her hips moved slow—deliberate. *Dry humping.*

"Can't fight it, can you?" Jessie murmured, lowering her mouth to Jenny's nipple, sucking gently, then sniffing again at her pit.

"God, you stink so *good.*"

Spank. A soft one. Then another. Jenny jolted slightly, tongue still hanging out.

"You like being broken."

Jessie took her time—fondling, licking, sniffing. Her lips grazed Jenny's belly, inner thigh, neck. The KO'd jobber was a canvas now, and Jessie was painting her dominance into every touch.

When it was done, Jessie stood tall. Jenny was nude, KO'd, and coated in the scent of surrender.

Jessie planted one foot on her chest, one hand on her own hip, the other tracing lazy circles around her own damp crotch.

"Pinned and perfect," she whispered.

Click.

A camera flash. Someone had been watching all along.

Story 1 — The Jobber's Downfall

Lesson: The Power of Sensual Domination & Trust

- **Tip:** Build tension slowly. Notice how Jessie uses gradual stripping, sniffing, and teasing to *mentally disarm* Jenny. Erotic domination isn't always about brute force—it's about reading your partner's reactions.
- **Consent Reminder:** All stripping, choking, and pinning scenes should be fully discussed beforehand. Safe signals (verbal or hand taps) are critical.
- **Sexual Health:** Long sessions of dry humping or body grinding can build core strength and release endorphins for both partners. Hydration and proper stretching before any physical play is highly recommended.

STORY 2 — *Roommates & Rivals*

Intro Preview:

The apartment smelled faintly of sweat and lotion—a subtle hint of what was about to unfold.

Two friends, two roommates, two women who had played this game in their minds long before today.

Alyssa, lithe and gym-tight, stretched on the living room mat, her sports bra barely containing her breathing chest. Across from her, **Vanessa** watched, arms crossed, eyes hungry behind her teasing grin.

What started as playful wrestling would soon evolve into something neither fully expected—**a slow surrender into limp, quivering arousal**.

In this space, with no rules and no audience, domination would simmer. Sweat would mingle with scent. Skin would touch skin in ways that blurred the line between combat and craving.

One would fall limp under the other's control, spread open for more than just a pin.

The real match hadn't even started yet.

Story 2: Roommates & Rivals

POV: Omniscient — watching the slow unraveling of playful tension between two roommates that turns into domination and sensual KO

The apartment was quiet, save for the hum of a fan and the soft shuffle of bare feet against hardwood.

Alyssa, a toned redhead with freckles and a gym rat's body, leaned on the back of the couch. Her sports bra was dark with sweat, and her tiny gym shorts barely covered her ass.

Across the living room, **Vanessa**, her roommate, wore nothing but a loose tank top and black bikini-cut panties. She was stretching—long, slow movements that felt suspiciously performative.

Alyssa grinned. "Still think you can take me?"

Vanessa raised a brow. "I know I can."

What started as a teasing challenge became a full-on *floor match*, right there in the living room.

Grappling turned to grinding. Playful taunts became sensual holds.

Alyssa trapped Vanessa in a side body scissors. Vanessa's moans were half-effort, half-pleasure. Her tank top slipped, revealing a hard nipple.

"That's one point for me," Alyssa teased, releasing her and letting her flop to the floor.

But Vanessa wasn't done. She lunged—**a surprise chokehold from behind**. Alyssa gasped, wriggled, then went still.

Vanessa lowered her gently to the carpet. Arms sprawled. Tongue slipping out. Chest heaving.

"Mmm… limp already?" she whispered, crawling over her.

She mounted Alyssa's belly, leaned forward, and *sniffed* her underarm deeply.

"Oh damn… sweaty little gym bunny."

She licked Alyssa's neck, trailing her tongue up to the jawline. Her fingers traced down Alyssa's abs, under the waistband of her shorts.

Alyssa twitched faintly.

"Oh you're *not* done yet, huh?"

She flipped her over, *spanked her ass*, hard. Alyssa groaned softly. Vanessa peeled the shorts down, revealing a soaked thong, and slid two fingers up the back of it, stroking.

"That's two points."

Another choke, softer this time. Alyssa's eyes fluttered. Then closed. Then her body went *still.*

Vanessa grinned, gently spreading her arms and legs into a perfect pin pose—face up now. She licked her fingers and traced slow circles on Alyssa's inner thigh.

She pressed her crotch against Alyssa's face and *dry humped* slowly, moaning.

"Mmm… that smell. That sweat. That *submission.*"

One hand fondled Alyssa's breast, the other slid between her own thighs as she rocked harder.

Alyssa twitched. Vanessa smiled.

“You’ll make such a good toy.”

She leaned down and kissed her KO’d roommate hard—wet, deep, possessive. Then she sniffed her armpit one more time and whispered:

“Hope you’re not planning on getting up.”

Story 2 — Roommates & Rivals

Lesson: Intimacy Grows in Playful Competition

- **Tip:** Erotic play wrestling can deepen intimacy between partners—especially with real-life friends exploring power dynamics. Start with light grappling, safe holds, and practice stillness during "pretend KO" to enhance trust.
- **Consent Reminder:** Always check in before introducing new sensations like armpit sniffing or spanking. Communication makes these kinks hotter and safer.
- **Sexual Health:** Light pressure holds (like playful chokeholds) increase adrenaline and sensitivity but require absolute trust and awareness of your partner's limits. Never hold breath-play positions without prior consent and extensive safety knowledge.

STORY 3 — *Model Mayhem*

Intro Preview:

The lights hummed like electric bees, casting a golden glow onto the photo studio's padded floor.

Carmen, flawless and oiled to a perfect gleam, adjusted her pose under the direction of the photographer. She had done shoots before—but none quite like this.

Behind the lens stood **Marina**. Cool. Controlled. **Dominant.**

Today was more than just photos. It was an audition of chemistry, consent, and quiet power.

As the shoot unfolded, the distance between model and photographer would dissolve.

What began as a simple pose would transform into a sensual scene of control, with Carmen lying limp beneath Marina's precise, hungry touch—**a living canvas for a dominant artist's desire**.

Story 3: Model Mayhem

POV: Omniscient voyeur — watching a photographer-model dynamic shift from professional to primal.

"Loosen your stance. That's it—hips just a little more forward. You're a knockout, baby."

The lights buzzed overhead as **Carmen**, a leggy Latina model in a cut-up sports bra and booty shorts, posed in front of a soft-padded floor backdrop. Her skin shimmered with baby oil, every inch gleaming under the heat of the shoot lamps.

Behind the camera stood **Marina**, the photographer—tall, cool, and calm, dressed in black jeans and a sheer crop top. She had the air of someone in control of everything.

"Now give me that cocky fighter pose," Marina purred, lifting her camera.

Carmen flexed, smirked—and then tripped into a staged fall. She landed back-first onto the mat, legs open slightly, tongue out.

"Oh my god," Marina whispered. "Hold that."

Click. Click.

Carmen stayed still. Then she giggled. "What, am I dead now?"

Marina lowered the camera.

"Almost," she murmured.

The shift was immediate. Marina stepped over Carmen's body, one knee to each side of her waist, pinning her.

"You like playing KO?" she asked softly.

Carmen's breath hitched. "Maybe…"

"Let's see how long you can hold still."

Marina leaned down and *sniffed* Carmen's armpit slowly, sighing like she just opened a bottle of aged wine.

"Mmm… that baby oil's hiding your real scent. You're musty underneath. I like that."

Carmen bit her lip, trying not to react.

Marina's fingers slid under her bra, tugged it up. A nipple popped free—Marina licked it. Then she kissed her way down to Carmen's belly, licked a slow line, and dipped into her shorts.

Carmen arched. Marina pushed her back down.

"Stay limp, baby. That's the rule."

She sat up, pulled Carmen's top off entirely. Shorts came next—tugged down slowly, deliberately.

Carmen now lay in nothing but a thong, oiled and gleaming, twitching in anticipation.

Marina pressed her crotch against Carmen's and began to **dry hump**, slow at first—just enough to rock their hips together.

"You look better like this," she murmured. "Beaten. Wet. Owned."

Another kiss. Then a **chokehold**, soft but firm. Carmen's breath caught—then slowed. Then stopped.

Her body went slack.

Marina spread her arms wide. Spread her legs. Tongue out. She posed her like a canvas.

"Perfect."

She sniffed both pits—*deeply*. Her fingers slid under Carmen's thong and rubbed gently.

"Let's make some art…"

Click.

The camera captured the moment: one model, limp and open. The other, wild-eyed and dripping, dominating her masterpiece.

Story 3 — Model Mayhem

Lesson: Sensuality Through Performance Kink

- **Tip:** Voyeuristic setups (camera recording, staged photoshoots) can amplify arousal by mixing fantasy with exhibitionism. Combine visual teasing (oiled skin, slow stripping) with verbal control.
- **Consent Reminder:** Using recording equipment requires explicit consent. Discuss beforehand whether the footage stays private, gets deleted, or is shared.
- **Sexual Health:** Kink scenes blending oil or lotions should use skin-safe, unscented products. Clean-up becomes part of the aftercare and can extend the erotic experience.

STORY 4 — *The KO Queen's Audition*

Intro Preview:

Brooke thought she was here for a simple custom shoot audition. Show her skills, get the job, play limp for the camera.

But **Lana**—her tester—had other plans.

The mat room was intimate, its padded floor promising softness even as the air grew heavy with tension.

This wasn't just a test of acting.

This was a test of **submission**.

As Brooke submitted to holds, strips, and whispered commands, her nerves gave way to something hotter: an unfamiliar ache of arousal at being so thoroughly controlled.

And Lana? She knew exactly how to guide a new girl into deeper, wetter surrender—**limp, pinned, possessed**.

Story 4: The KO Queen's Audition

POV: Omniscient voyeur — watching a new girl get introduced to a kinkier world than she expected.

"You've done shoots before?"

"A few," said **Brooke**, trying to sound confident. She stood barefoot on the edge of a private mat room—small, soundproofed, dimly lit. Her white tank top clung to her tight chest, her athletic shorts already riding up. She looked *ready*. But her voice betrayed the nervous flutter in her belly.

Across from her stood **Lana**, older, more experienced, calm like a panther. Her one-piece was cut low at the chest, legs bare and glistening. She circled Brooke like she was shopping.

"This isn't *just* a shoot," Lana said, low and husky. "This is a test."

Brooke blinked. "A… test?"

"You said you wanted to work in customs. That you could act limp. Take a KO. Handle some… touching."

Brooke nodded slowly. "Yeah. I mean, I think I can—"

Lana's arms wrapped around her in a flash. A **bearhug**, tight and sensual. Brooke gasped. Lana whispered into her ear.

"Then show me."

Brooke writhed for a second… then went limp.

Lana lowered her gently to the mat, straddled her belly, and **spread her arms wide**.

“Good girl,” she purred. “But I need more.”

She lifted Brooke’s shirt up and over her head. No bra. Lana whistled softly.

“Now we’re warming up.”

A **straddle pin** followed, Lana sitting heavy on her hips, slowly **grinding** her crotch forward. She leaned down, sniffed one of Brooke’s armpits.

“Mmm… already musty. Nervous sweat.”

She slapped Brooke’s cheek gently.

“Stay limp.”

Then she leaned down, sucked Brooke’s nipple, and whispered filth into her ear. Brooke twitched, tongue slipping out unconsciously.

“Look at that…” Lana giggled. “Already drooling. And we haven’t even *started.*”

A slow **DDT** left Brooke splayed on her back, twitching slightly. Lana tugged down her shorts, revealing tight pink panties already damp between the thighs.

Lana licked her lips. “You smell like someone who needs to be pinned.”

She slipped a hand into Brooke’s panties and rubbed gently. Her other hand lifted an arm and **sniffed her again**, slower this time.

“Yup. That’s it. Perfectly stinky.”

Lana **spanked** her hard. Brooke groaned—*still limp.*

“You’re gonna make us money, little KO queen.”

The final hold was a **reverse face-sit pin**, Lana grinding her ass down on Brooke's face while gripping both thighs. She moaned low as she humped slow and steady.

Brooke twitched. Her arms spread. Her legs kicked once.

Then stillness.

Lana didn't stop humping for another full minute.

When she rose, Brooke's face was flushed, her tongue out, her hair a mess.

Lana crouched, kissed her forehead, then whispered:

"Audition passed."

Story 4 — The KO Queen's Audition

Lesson: Guiding Beginners into Submission Play

- **Tip:** Introducing someone new to KO play means emphasizing **gradual trust-building**. Start with short holds, careful observation of their breathing, and regular check-ins.
- **Consent Reminder:** Auditions or training scenarios must always be transparent. Surprise moves can only happen with prior agreement to "surprise zones" or red/yellow/green safe words.
- **Sexual Health:** Sensual domination can lower cortisol (stress hormone) and increase oxytocin (bonding hormone). Proper aftercare—physical and emotional—reinforces trust and enhances future play.

STORY 5 — *The Ring Is Hers*

Intro Preview:

The ring had seen countless matches. But tonight?

It would witness **total erotic conquest**.

Dana, the boss, had ruled the roster for years—never stepping between the ropes herself.

Until tonight.

And **Reese**?

Young. Dangerous. Ready.

Under the harsh spotlight, power would shift. Clothes would peel away. Bodies would tangle.

And in the end, Dana would be left completely limp, exposed, and twitching under Reese's rhythmic, hungry grinding—**stripped of everything but sweat, surrender, and the taste of defeat**.

Story 5: The Ring Is Hers

POV: Omniscient voyeur — witnessing the ultimate downfall of a powerful woman who thought she was in control.

"You sure you don't need a warm-up?"

The gym lights dimmed over the ring, casting long shadows on the mat.

Dana, the promoter—tough, built, bossy—was tightening her gloves, smirking at the woman across from her. She wore a cropped tank, sheer compression shorts, and full attitude.

Reese, the younger wrestler, didn't flinch. She was lean and lethal, with a look in her eyes that said *you're already mine.* Her red singlet hugged every curve, her boots laced high.

"You've been barking orders long enough," Reese said, rolling her shoulders. "Time for someone to put you in your place."

Dana laughed. "You think *you're* gonna break me?"

The bell rang—unofficially, a gesture more than a sound.

Reese struck fast—**a knee to the belly**, followed by a swift **snapmare** that left Dana stunned on her back. She tried to get up—**DDT**. Down again.

"Getting sleepy already, boss?" Reese cooed.

Dana crawled for the ropes, but Reese straddled her back, reached down, and **sniffed**.

"Mmm… sweaty, angry… musty." She smirked. "My favorite kind."

She peeled Dana's tank top up and over her head, exposing her chest—bare, full, already flushed.

A **belly splash** followed. Dana grunted, arms falling to her sides.

Reese unzipped Dana's shorts, dragging them down slowly, revealing **nothing underneath.**

"Wow. Were you planning to be pinned today?"

Dana twitched but didn't respond.

Reese straddled her again—*grinding*. Her hips rocked slowly over Dana's slick skin. She leaned down and began **kissing her belly**, **licking her breasts**, **sniffing her pits**, moaning low the whole time.

"Oh, you *reek* of submission now."

One **spank. Two. Three.** Dana moaned, limp.

Her legs were spread, arms posed wide. Her **tongue lolled out**, eyes glassy.

Reese stood for a moment, slowly stripped off her singlet—now nude except for her boots.

"Time to finish this…"

She lowered herself into a **face-sit**, but reversed—her ass grinding down onto Dana's nose and mouth, crotch gliding across her chin.

Dry humping, slow at first, then faster.

"Ohh yeah… yeah, you *take it.*"

She reached back and slapped Dana's thigh.

"Still twitching. Good girl."

The match ended not with a bell, but with a moan. Reese collapsed across Dana's body, panting, licking her own fingers.

Dana didn't move. Her limbs were splayed wide, her body used, her chest rising slow.

Reese whispered into her ear.

"This ring belongs to me now."

Then she kissed her KO'd opponent long and deep, leaving her lip-gloss mark on Dana's open mouth.

Story 5 — The Ring Is Hers

Lesson: Erotic Humiliation & Total Control

- **Tip:** Full stripping, face-sitting, and long dry-humping pins combine humiliation with intense arousal. These scenes work best when your partner fully embraces surrender.
- **Consent Reminder:** Never assume your partner enjoys humiliation—explicitly negotiate beforehand. Allow aftercare space for emotional processing.
- **Sexual Health:** Extended grinding and heavy face-sitting may cause temporary numbness or soreness; communicate any discomfort immediately. Staying hydrated and ensuring clear airways during heavy pins are crucial safety priorities.

Epilogue: The Afterglow

There's something beautiful about surrender—not just the physical act of going limp beneath someone, but the mental release, the emotional softness, the permission to **let go**.

If you've made it to the end of *Pinned & Possessed Vol. 1*, chances are you're someone who understands, or is starting to explore, the thrill of power exchange. Whether you're a curious reader, a performer, a dominant, a submissive, or somewhere fluid in between—you've now stepped into a world where **wrestling isn't just about strength. It's about sensuality, scent, breath, control… and trust.**

These stories were crafted to ignite fantasies, but they're grounded in real kink dynamics. In every pin, every chokehold, every slow grind or armpit sniff, there's a layer of **negotiated play** underneath the surface. **Fetish exploration should always be safe, consensual, and rooted in mutual pleasure.**

If you find yourself aroused by these scenes, that's not just normal—it's natural. Your body responds to **stimulation, vulnerability, and anticipation**, and fetishes like limp play, erotic wrestling, and domination are simply extensions of how we explore those sensations.

There are benefits, too:

- **Deeper intimacy** with partners when trust is built through safe control.
- **Stress release** as the submissive body surrenders tension.
- **Increased body awareness** and confidence for dominants and submissives alike.
- And sometimes, just the sheer joy of dripping sweat, panting breath, and that dizzy warmth after a hard pin.

But with this kind of intensity comes responsibility:

- Always establish **boundaries, safe words, and aftercare needs.**
- Never assume someone enjoys humiliation or KO fantasy—**ask first.**
- Understand the risks of things like **chokeholds or breath play**, and never play recklessly.
- Make **space for recovery**—physically and emotionally—after scenes.

As *Phantom Rose*, I write these stories not just to make you hard, wet, or breathless—but to make you **feel seen**. To celebrate the bodies, minds, and emotions involved in kink. To bring something filthy and fantastic into the realm of artistry.

What Comes Next...

This is only the beginning.

In *Pinned & Possessed Vol. 2*, the heat will rise. We'll explore new arenas, more complex dynamics, and even **deeper forms of domination and surrender.**

Expect:

- New characters—rookies, veterans, and rivals.
- Fetishes layered into limp wrestling: **body worship, strap-on pinning, sensory deprivation, even light bondage mixed with KO play.**
- Longer matches, **more stripping**, **darker power games**, and **new fantasies you didn't even know you had**.

Volume 1 was about introduction, foreplay, and first blood.

Volume 2?

That's where we take off the gloves… and the panties.

— Phantom Rose 🌹

www.ingramcontent.com/pod-product-compliance
Lightning Source LLC
LaVergne TN
LVHW020313110826
845148LV00017BA/2668

* 9 7 9 8 2 1 8 7 4 4 6 7 0 *